Leif's Saga

Leif's Saga

A Viking Tale

by Jonathan Hunt

Simon & Schuster Books for Young Readers

SIMON & SCHUSTER BOOKS FOR YOUNG READERS
An imprint of Simon & Schuster Children's Publishing Division, 1230 Avenue of the
Americas, New York, New York 10020. Copyright © 1996 by Jonathan Hunt. All
rights reserved including the right of reproduction in whole or in part in any form.
SIMON & SCHUSTER BOOKS FOR YOUNG READERS is a trademark of Simon &
Schuster. Book design by Anahid Hamparian. The text of this book is set in 15-point
Phaistos Roman. The illustrations are rendered in transparent watercolors and acrylics
on 140-lb hot-pressed rag paper. The paintings were color separated by laser scanner
and reproduced using magenta, cyan, yellow, and black inks. Manufactured in the
United States of America
First Edition 10 9 8 7 6 5 4 3 2 1
Library of Congress Cataloging-in-Publication Data
Hunt, Jonathan.
    Leif's Saga / by Jonathan Hunt. — 1st American ed.
    p.   cm.
Summary: A Viking boatbuilder tells his daughter the story of Leif Ericson's
voyage to and discovery of North America.
    ISBN 0-689-80492-X
    1. Leiv Eiriksson, d. ca. 1020—Juvenile fiction.   [1. Ericson, Leif, d. ca. 1020—
Fiction.   2. Vikings—Fiction.]   I. Title.
PZ7.H91564Le   1996   [Fic]—dc20   94-14233   CIP   AC

ACKNOWLEDGMENTS

I would like to extend my heartfelt thanks to: Clayton Colbourne
of Parks Canada, guide and storyteller extraordinaire, for
touching the bright spark of life to the embers of the past. Bella E.
Hodge, owner of the appropriately named Valhalla Lodge, for
sharing tales of restless ghosts and a certain amber pendant,
and for serving Newfoundland's best pancakes with bakeapple
sauce. Åke Koel, who shared his extensive knowledge of Norse
history and language by offering comments on the original
manuscript for *Leif's Saga*, and Odd S. Lovoll, Ph.D.,King
Olav V Professor of Scandinavian-American Studies at
St. Olaf College, for his expert reading of my text and his
careful review of my original paintings. Wayne Murrin
of Parks Canada, who answered my endless questions and
somehow found the time to hunt up and photocopy
archaeological articles for me. I also wish to express my
appreciation to everyone on the staff of the L'Anse aux
Meadows National Historic Park for their enthusiastic
assistance. And last, but not least, I would like to thank
my editor, Virginia Duncan, for believing in this
project from the very beginning. Without all of you,
Leif's Saga would have been just another story.

This one also is for Lisa, with my love

$\mathcal{S}$IGRID pushed past the heavy skin that hung in the doorway and stumbled into the shed along with a flurry of snow. Asgrim looked up from his work, and his frown quickly melted into a smile when he saw his daughter.

"How is your work going, Poppa?" she asked.

Asgrim ran his hand proudly along the planks of the hull. The boat was a compact and sturdy knörr, designed to hold supplies for long voyages—not at all like the graceful longships of the Viking warriors.

"The knörr will be ready to sail by spring," he assured her. "I do not think I could wait much longer, for the magic locked in this wood is strong."

"Magic?" said Sigrid, frowning at the drab planks.

"Oh, yes," answered her father. "The strongest kind."

"Where will you sail, Poppa?" Sigrid asked. "Will you find treasures and fight sea monsters?"

"You have many questions for a girl! Why aren't you back at the house with the women?" Sigrid's father teased.

"Oh, Poppa! All they do is sit at their looms and gossip about everyone in the village. I have so much more fun being with you and listening to your stories."

Asgrim swept Sigrid up in a bear hug and kissed her on the cheek. She giggled and squirmed at the tickle of his mustache.

"Would you like me to tell a story now, Red?"

"Would you, Poppa?" Asgrim grinned and plopped his daughter down on top of a barrel.

Sigrid's eyes danced with anticipation as Asgrim leaned comfortably against the gunwale of the knörr and began his tale.

✠ ✠ ✠

"EIRIK the Red and his wife, Thjodhild, were the first to settle here in Greenland. Leif was the eldest of their three sons. Leif was full of questions and longed for a life of adventure.

"Life was hard in Greenland, so during the spring and summer months, Eirik hired on a crew and sailed off to trade and hunt. He would return to his family at the end of summer, the hold of his knörr stuffed with gifts and provisions, and Eirik himself close to bursting with stories and news of the world. Leif would sit up all night listening to tales of warriors, monsters, and far-off lands.

"One time, Eirik told of how a sea trader named Bjarne Herfjolfsson had been blown far to the west by a storm. When the waves settled and the sky cleared, he sighted three mysterious coasts. But Bjarne was not a curious man, and he never set foot upon those shores. Young Leif's imagination ran wild at the thought of these unexplored lands.

"When he was nineteen, Leif journeyed from his home at Brattahlid to Bjarne's farm, where he was warmly welcomed. After the evening meal, Leif listened intently to Bjarne's tale and memorized every detail. Early the next morning, Leif thanked his host and left for home.

"When he arrived back at Brattahlid, Leif begged his father to accompany him as leader of an expedition to rediscover Bjarne's lands. With Eirik's seagoing experience, Leif felt sure that they would succeed. Father and son spent the long winter overhauling Eirik's knörr and gathering supplies for the journey.

"At last, the grinding crags of ice that pack the winter fjords of Greenland melted. The knörr was uncovered and dragged down to the rocky beach. But Eirik fell and broke his arm as he and Leif walked down the steep path to the fjord. In the end, it was decided that Tyrkir, Leif's foster father, would go in place of Eirik. But Leif would be leader of the expedition.

"The water was like a sheet of burnished silver when the knörr sped off into the western sea, with Leif at the rudder.

"When the familiar rocky bluffs of Greenland had disappeared from view, Leif navigated by the sun and stars.

"After sailing for four days and three nights, the crew was startled by Leif's shout of 'Land!' The explorers had reached the first of the three coasts. When Leif set foot upon the beach, he gazed about and saw only tumbled and broken stones.

"'Even the dwarfs and frost giants have forsaken this place! I will call it Helluland, Flatstone Land,' he said.

"Leif returned to the knörr, and the anchor was weighed.

"After a few more days of sailing, they sighted the next coast. Leif marveled at the sloping white beaches and mist-shrouded forests.

"'Proud and mighty ships will one day be wrought from these magnificent trees! I will call this place Markland, Forestland.'

"At Leif's order, the knörr once again set sail. They sailed through two days and a night, following the last of Bjarne's directions. At twilight on the second day, the air was alive with the call of birds, and Leif knew that land again was near.

"A shout of joy went up from the crew when a small island appeared before them. The knörr was brought in close, and the salt-stiff sail was taken down. The men clambered over the sides and splashed through the shallows to get ashore. Birds rose up from the beach in flapping, squawking clouds. There were so many nests of eggs in the sand that there was hardly room to take a step!

"Leif knelt to taste the dew on the grass, and it seemed to him that nothing had ever tasted so sweet. Leif had his crew lay out their sleeping skins, and they passed their first night in the new land.

"In the morning, they returned to the knörr and rowed it into a harbor that appeared carved into the coast of the mainland. It was here Leif decided to build winter dwellings for himself and his crew.

"The bounty of game and fish that they caught was unlike anything they had ever seen in Greenland. It did not take long to salt and smoke enough meat to last them through the coming winter months.

"Throughout the spring and summer, Leif split his crew into two parties. One group of men explored the sun-dappled forest, while the rest remained at camp. The men marveled at every new mushroom, animal, and tree that they discovered.

"Late one day, men rushed into Leif's hut. Tyrkir had disappeared! Leif called all the men together, and they searched the forest. The next morning, they found the old fellow wandering lost, his tunic torn and leaves tangled in his beard.

"'Were you attacked?' blurted Leif.

"'Oh, no,' Tyrkir smiled. 'There is not a soul but us living in this paradise. I merely did some exploring on my own—and this is what I have found!' Tyrkir reached into his belt pouch and pulled out a handful of plump berries. 'With these we can make wine!'

"'I shall call this place Vinland!' Leif shouted. And Wineland it was from that time onward.

"After the harsh winters and short summers of Greenland, this new land truly was a paradise. But Leif knew they would have to return home to tell everyone of the wonders they had found.

"The knörr was packed from bow to stern with dried fish, meat and skins, fresh water, and berries. Leif also directed his men to fell a number of straight and sturdy oaks, for good wood was scarce back home.

"They disembarked on a day when the sea and sky were bright and clear. Leif pointed the bow out to sea, and a steady wind filled the knörr's sail. When Leif gazed back at the rapidly receding coast of Vinland, his heart was filled with a longing to someday return.

"Just as they reached safe harbor in Greenland, the sky grew heavy with black clouds that tarnished the sea and cast an eerie light over the adventurers. The crew whispered of ill omens but kept to their duties.

"Suddenly, a great cheer went up from the shore. The families of Leif and his crew had come down to the beach to greet them! Everyone had tales to tell, and the sounds of joyful reunions echoed up and down the fjord.

"The feasting at Brattahlid lasted many days and nights as stories of Vinland's endless summers and bountiful game were told and retold.

"But when the celebrations had ended, Eirik grew ill. It was not long before the old adventurer died quietly in his bed with his family by his side.

"As the eldest son, it now fell to Leif to see his family safely through the bitter winter. When spring once again came to Greenland, Leif was too burdened by responsibilities to even think of returning to Vinland.

"A brave few did try to trace Leif's course back to Vinland. Many were lost in storms and never heard from again. Men grew reluctant to leave their families to risk the journey.

"Leif made wine from the berries he had brought back from Vinland. He shared this wine with only his most honored guests. The oak logs he kept for many years, in the hopes that one day he might build a new ship and return to Vinland. But over time, his dream faded like a snowflake melts into the sea. Leif had to sell the oak to pay for winter supplies."

✠ ✠ ✠

SGRIM paused. When he continued, his voice was heavy with emotion.

"I bought that wood, Red, and used it to build this boat." Asgrim bowed his head, ending the tale.

Sigrid reached out and touched the rough-hewn planks. Suddenly, she was able to see the magic in the wood. As the boat was taking shape under her father's hand, the splinters of one man's lost dream were being wrought anew. For long moments, Sigrid sat in awed silence.

"Poppa," she said at last. "Teach me to sail the great sea. Then you and I can go to Vinland together!"

Asgrim raised his eyebrows at the determination in his daughter's voice.

"Red," he confided with a proud smile, "I never intended to leave without you."

A NOTE FROM THE AUTHOR

The ancient Norse earned a reputation for being a restless, wandering people, and they well deserved this distinction. Although the Vikings were fierce warriors, they were no more bloodthirsty than the average knights of the Middle Ages. In fact, medieval Englishmen thought it odd that before going out for a night on the town, Viking warriors would bathe and then comb their hair and beards! It is also a myth that Vikings wore horned helmets into battle. This false notion was probably inspired by the imaginative engravings of nineteenth-century illustrators and then perpetuated by many modern fantasy artists.

During the eighth century, Swedes eager for booty and trade obtainable in the Far East traveled along the mighty rivers of Russia and reached the Black and Caspian seas. In fact, Russia was named after this particular group of Swedes, who were called the Rus. Danish and Norwegian sailors went *a-viking* (adventuring or pirating) from the North Sea to the northern tip of Africa. In between, they sacked, looted, and captured slaves, and established settlements in Spain, England, and France.

The Norwegians set up numerous trading outposts and colonies as they made their way westward. Some of these settlements included the Shetland, Hebrides, and Faeroe islands (bits and pieces of the ancient Norse language survive in the dialects of these regions even today). They also established kingdoms in Ireland and France, as well as colonies in Iceland and Greenland. There are many possible explanations for the explosive migration of the Norse people in the late eighth century. More likely than not it was a combination of many factors that contributed to the rise in Viking activity.

Banishment, or outlawry, was a severe punishment dealt out at the *Althing* (a yearly assembly of freemen where laws were enacted and punishments carried out). One result of these banishments was that many of the accused men left with their families and started farms in new lands while in exile. Leif's father, Eirik the Red, discovered and named Greenland after having been outlawed from Iceland.

The Norse were a fiercely proud and self-sufficient people, and many *bondi* (independent landowners) resented the strong-willed kings who were, at that time, attempting to consolidate Scandinavia into distinct countries with centralized governments. Many *bondi* reacted by packing up their families and leaving their homes in search of new lands to farm.

These incredible migrations were made possible by the flexible trading craft called *knörrs*. These masterfully designed vessels were constructed from the outside in by lashing and nailing together a lightweight shell of overlapping, wedge-shaped oak planks that were then reinforced by transverse ribs. The steering board, or rudder, was affixed to the rear right-hand side of the craft. *Stjornbordi*, the Norse word for "steering board," eventually evolved into our word "starboard." When it came to nautical navigation, the Norse were renowned throughout the medieval world. There were no maps, so a Scandinavian seaman relied almost entirely upon memory and an intimate knowledge of the sea to guide his craft. He could tell how far he was from land by the color of the water, as well as the size and shape of waves and ice floes.

It was not just skill that led many Norsemen to new lands; luck had a hand in this too. According to the sagas, Iceland, Greenland, and North America were each discovered by the Norse purely by chance when a ship was blown off course in bad weather!

The historical basis for *Leif's Saga* can be found in the Icelandic *Eirik the Red's Saga* and the *Greenlanders' Saga*. According to Gwyn Jones in his book *Eirik the Red and Other Icelandic Sagas*, the word *saga* means "'something said,' something recorded in words, and hence by easy extension a prose story or narrative." The Icelandic sagas were originally passed down as oral histories of families and events, which were not written down until hundreds of years after they were first told!

Historians estimate that Leif Eiriksson's voyage took place around the year 1000. At that time, the average temperature of northern North America and southern Greenland was one to four degrees higher than it is today. This means the fjords and bays that remain choked with drift ice well into summer today were probably almost ice-free in the spring when the Vikings set out to sea. This allowed the Scandinavians more time to explore before they were forced to return home or build winter shelters. This warm climatic cycle also helps to explain why Leif's men did not encounter any native peoples during their explorations. The Inuit would have followed game north into the colder regions.

One aspect of the sagas that has been a source of contention for generations of scholars is the actual geographical locations of Leif's Helluland, Markland, and most especially, Vinland. Using descriptions from the sagas and matching them to known locations, experts have tentatively established Helluland as the southern tip of Baffin Island and Markland as Porcupine Strand, in Labrador. The most controversy has erupted over the location of Vinland.

The etymology of the name Vinland alone has been the cause of much confusion and disagreement. For centuries, scholars translated *Vinland* as "Wineland" because, according to earlier translations of the sagas, Leif found grapes there. Newer and more thoughtful translations, however, are more specific in stating that Leif found not grapes but *vinber* (wineberries), which could mean anything from gooseberries to currants or bakeapples (also called cloudberries). This newer theory has also cast doubt on the notion that Vinland could only be situated as far north as the northern-most range of wild grapes.

Estimates as to the location of Vinland have ranged from Labrador all the way to Florida! However, the only substantiated Norse discoveries in North America were uncovered at L'Anse aux Meadows in northern Newfoundland by Helge Ingstad, with the help of the local fishing community, in 1960. Ingstad insists that the remains of the structures and artifacts he and his wife, archaeologist Anne Stine, have unearthed are of Norse origin and are, more specifically, Leif's *búðir* (booths, or winter dwellings) as described in the sagas. There are few who refute Ingstad and Stine's supposition. The only real questions that remain unanswered are these: For how long were the structures occupied before they were eventually abandoned, and are there any more sites that have yet to be rediscovered?

During the week of August 27 through September 3, 1993, my wife, Lisa, and I visited the L'Anse aux Meadows site so I could complete my research for *Leif's Saga*. There I experienced firsthand the conditions that helped to mold the disposition and character of the ancient Norse.

While walking the wooden boardwalk over the bakeapple-studded peat bog, our umbrella was blown inside out by blasts of wind from Epaves Bay. Beyond the bay and across the Strait of Belle Isle, I could vaguely make out the coast of Labrador as a gray smudge on the mist-shrouded horizon. The rain and hail that pelted us felt like blunt needles. After a walk of no more than three or four hundred yards, we were shivering and dripping wet. We spent the next couple of hours steaming in front of a smokey fire in the reconstructed sod and timber longhouse, listening as a guide related facts and spun stories about the men and women who had lived and worked in that harsh place almost one thousand years ago. I could not imagine a better way to spend an afternoon!

A local woman told me about a carved, triangular piece of amber set in a worked metal mounting and suspended from a chain, which had been found by the woman's grandmother at the L'Anse aux Meadows site. This was long before the outside world knew about the existence of the Norse ruins buried there. The amber pendant, I was told, was eventually lost in a fire without ever having been revealed to and authenticated by archaeologists. Jewelry of this type was common among Norse men and women, so I took the liberty to show Leif himself wearing the mysterious amber pendant.

As time goes on, it becomes more clear to us how medieval people viewed the world around them. Thanks in large part to the legacy of the roaming Scandinavians, educated people of medieval Europe had begun to see the world as a sphere and not a flat surface from which one could fall.

A NOTE ON THE RUNES

The mysterious letters that can be found throughout *Leif's Saga* are called *runes* (from *rūn*, the ancient Norse word for "mystery"). The Norse believed that their alphabet had been passed down to them and instilled with magical powers by the god Odin. Some scholars have theorized that runes originated in the mountainous regions of northern Italy in the first century B.C. By 200 A.D., the use of runes had spread to Scandinavia. The runes used in *Leif's Saga* are based on the Swedo-Norwegian *futhork* (named after the first six letters of the alphabet).

ᛉ	ᚢ	ᚦ	ᚨ	ᚱ	ᚴ	•	ᚼ	ᚾ	ᛁ	ᛅ	ᛦ	•	ᛋ	ᛏ	ᛒ	ᛘ	ᛚ
f	u	th	o	r	k	•	h	n	i	a	R	•	s	t	b	m	l

The messages in some of these paintings use these characters to spell out the sounds of English words. Since the Norse alphabet was limited to sixteen characters, it was sometimes necessary for me to make substitutions for missing letters (for example, the letter "j" is represented by ᛁ). Happy decoding!

SELECTED BIBLIOGRAPHY

Almgren, Bertil. *The Viking*. Gothenburg, Sweden: AB Nordbok, 1975.

Evans, Cheryl, and Anne Millard. *Usborne Illustrated Guide to Norse Myths and Legends*, illus. Rodney Matthews. Tulsa, OK: EDC Publishing, 1987.

Constable, George, ed. *Fury of the Northmen: TimeFrame AD 800–1000*. Alexandria, VA: Time-Life Books Inc., 1988.

Ingstad, Helge. *Land Under the Pole Star*, trans. Naomi Walford. New York: St. Martin's Press, 1966.

Jones, Gwyn. *Eirik the Red and Other Icelandic Sagas*. New York: Oxford University Press, 1986.

——. *The Norse Atlantic Saga*. New York: Oxford University Press, 1986.

La Fay, Howard. *The Vikings*. Washington, D.C.: National Geographic Society, 1972.

Magnusson, Magnus. *Iceland Saga*. London: The Bodley Head, 1987.

Neersø, Niels. *A Viking Ship: "Roar Ege"—A Reconstruction of a Trading Vessel from the Viking Age*. St. John's Newfoundland: Breakwater, 1986.

Oxenstierna, Eric. *The Norsemen*, trans. Catherine Hutter. Connecticut: New York Graphic Society Publishers, Ltd., 1965.

Simpson, Jacqueline. *The Viking World*. New York: St. Martin's Press, 1980.

Wernick, Robert, ed. *The Vikings*. Alexandria, VA: Time-Life Books Inc., 1988.

ARTICLES

Wallace, Birgitta Linderoth. "The L'Anse aux Meadows Buildings: Interpretation of the Archaeological Data." Prepared for use on the L'Anse aux Meadows Site, 1992.

——. "L'Anse aux Meadows: Gateway to Vinland." *Acta Archaeologica: The Norse of the North Atlantic*, Vol. 61 (1990): 166–97.